THE TOWN OF SUMPKINVILLE

PRESENTS

SIMON'S BATTY IMAGINATION

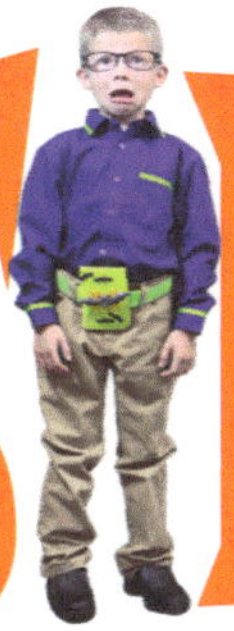

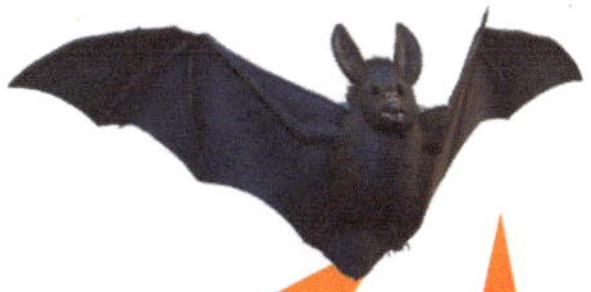

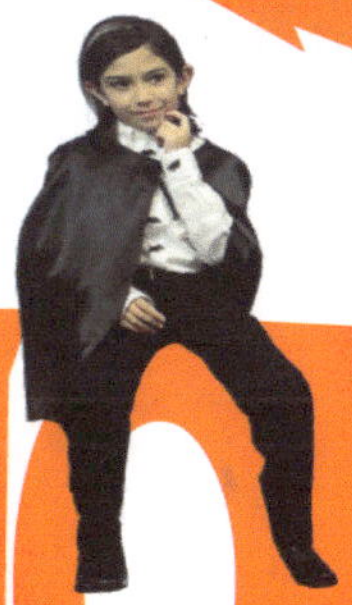

Written By Carmen Andersen

The town of Sumpkinville, as you know, has many magical shops and places that it is famous for.

One of the many wonders is the Looking Glass Tree. At night, the town folk gather to see the moonlight it mimics with its leaves. Some people say that the moonlight from this tree is the most marvelous thing that they have ever seen.

With all the magic and mystery the town offers, it's no surprise that some visitors decide, to make Sumpkinville their home, and so over the years the town has grown.

With so many visitors settling in, children need a place to stay while their parents are at work, and there is no place like Vladimir's Vizard Academy (V.V.A.).

Mr. Vladimir was saying just the other day, "The V.V.A. is a perfect place for children to come and play." Of course the V.V.A. is home to many kids, but today we are only going to talk about Simon and his friends.

Let's start with a young girl who loves to
dress up and play.

Her parents call her Alice, but she calls
herself Princess Alice. Alice dreams of
being a princess, not an ordinary princess, of
course, but a magical princess.

Princess Alice will one day reign over
Sumpkinville while riding her very own magical
unicorn.

Next, there is Captain Cutter who loves to
eat butter.

Every day he wears what he thinks is
a   magical cape, but what he doesn't know
is that he is actually wearing his Grandma's
pillow case.

HICCUP

Then of course, there is Herbert but his friends call him HIC.

"Why HIC?" you ask.

Well it's as simple as this.

Herbert hiccups when he gets scared, and unfortunately everything scares HIC. You should know though that there is more to HIC than his hiccups; he is also a kind and loyal friend.

Last, but certainly not least is, Simon who is the leader of the pack.

He is the one who decides what games to play, and that usually depends on what book he is reading that day. You see Simon loves to read and always shares his new books with his friends.

Sumpkinville
GUIDE
TO
VAMPIRES

MR VLADMIR CLASSROOM
PUMPKINVILLE
GUIDE TO VAMPIRES
NO GARLIC
NO REFLECTION
DRINK BLOOD

Today is "Sharing Day," and the children are not surprised that Simon has brought a new book. Simon proudly introduces **Sumpkinville's Guide to Vampires** and goes on to explain, "Most folks don't know that some vampires call **Sumpkinville** their home."

"Actually,if you look close, you will find that **Sumpkinville** is home to creatures of all kinds, but in this guide you will find everything you need to know about Vampires. Garlic makes them sick; they have no reflection in the mirror; and they drink blood every day of the year." Simon warns everyone.

As Simon is carrying on and on about everything he has learned, he looks over and sees something he has never seen before-- Mr. Vladimir drinking a bubbly cup of what he thinks can only be blood.

MR VLADMIR CLASSROOM
NO GARLIC
NO REFLECTION
DRINK BLOOD
SUMPKINVIIIE
GUIDE
TO
VAMPIRES

After sharing time ends, Simon can't wait to
find his friends.

"Mr. Vladimir is a vampire!" Simon reports
and he goes on to tell his friends how he saw
him drinking something bubbly and red.

"Simon's book is creepy. There is no such thing as a vampire.

Everyone has a reflection," Alice thinks to herself while she is busy playing dress up.

Suddenly, Alice panics when she looks up and notices that she does not see Mr. Vladimir's reflection where it should be.

Prissy Me

EAT
FOOD
BEFORE IT EATS YOU!!!
BUTTER

Later that day at lunch, Captain Cutter hears
all about Alice's tale of what she saw naught.

As Cutter eats and spreads more icky-licky
butter on his moldy garlic bread (A Spoogetti
and Meatballs specialty) he has a thought,
"What if I ask Mr. Vladimir to eat some of
my garlic bread?"

So Captain Cutter, brave as can be,
offers him a piece of his bread to eat, but
immediately Mr. Vladimir pinches his nose and
shakes his head.

Cutter is starting to believe.

EAT
FOOD
BEFORE IT EATS YOU!!

On the playground during recess, the kids gather
and share what they have learned.

Herbert says, while hiccuping only twice,
"I think Simon might be right:"

As they talk about everything they have seen,
their group starts to grow by two, then three.

Suddenly they realize that everyone on the
playground is listening.

MR VLADMIR CLASSROOM

After recess, Simon sits in class and thinks to himself, "I don't know what I should do. I should tell Mrs. Vladimir, but she could be a vampire too."
Just then, he hears Mrs. Vladimir voice on the intercom, "Simon, report to the office immediately!"

Simon, a bit confused, starts walking, but as he passes each kid, one desk at a time, what he sees is frightening. His friends are terrified for him. Confused no more, Simon is now scared to walk out the classroom door.

Just outside the creepy office door, Simon waits, and then waits some more when he realizes, "I have never been to the office before, and I have no idea what is behind that door!

Is it a cave? Will there be coffins on the floor?" Just then he hears Mrs. Vladimir say in a very creepy way, "Enter Simon, and don't delay!"

Slowly, Simon walks into the office, nervous but curious too. Since he has learned so much about vampires, he thinks, "I think it could be cool if vampires ran the school."

THE OFFICE

Simon's mind changes quickly, when he sees, Mrs. Vladimir glaring at him in the most hair-raising, spine-chilling way! At once the silent creepy glare is broken as Mrs. Vladimir clears her throat and asks, "Simon, can you tell me why the entire school thinks that Mr. Vladimir is a vampire?"

Fearful, Simon answers, "Well, it's because I saw Mr. Vladimir drinking something red; Alice couldn't see his reflection in her mirror; and then he wouldn't eat any garlic bread."

Mrs. Vladimir laughs loudly in a very eerie way. "Simon, Mr. Vladimir is not feeling well today. That red liquid you saw him drink was actually his medicine, and Mr. Vladimir has never liked garlic bread. As for his reflection, I cannot say, but it seems like once again your imagination has gotten the best of you."

After Mrs. Vladimir explains everything, Simon understands that it was because of him that this rumor started and then spread around the entire school. Disappointed in himself, Simon sighs and says "I'm sorry, Mrs. Vladimir, I promise to tell everyone the truth."

Simon leaves the office and goes to the Looking Glass Tree where he and his friends usually meet. They are all anxiously waiting for him.

Simon takes a deep breath and then tells them everything.

Later that day after all the children went home, Mrs. Vladimir said to Mr. Vladimir "Whew, that was a close call today.

Your drink almost gave us away!"

Mr. Vladimir simply replies "**BWAHAHA**"

FAN PAGES

Landon Denton is 7 years old. Landon wants to be the United States President when he grows up. He loves to read, play Minecraft, and play outside on his family farm. Landon is a sweet, silly, smart kid who likes to wear green.

LANDON DENTON

ZOEY MENCHEY

Zoe Grace Menchey is 6 years old and has aspirations of being a swimmer when she grows up. Zoe is an inquisitive, loving and outgoing little girl who loves to read, and play soccer and board games.

Keane Michael Rhodes is 6 years old and loves playing football. Keane likes dinosaurs and wants to be an archeologists when he grows up. At home, Keane likes to read and play with his three dogs.

KEANE RHODES

Cash S. Flippen is 6 years old and in 1st grade. He enjoys building with Legos and playing Minecraft. Cash is very helpful to others and is always caring towards his friends.

Jordan D. Finch is 9 years old and wants to be in the entertainment industry. She loves dressing up, acting, singing, dancing and drawing. She is a loving, sweet and caring young lady who loves being a social butterfly.

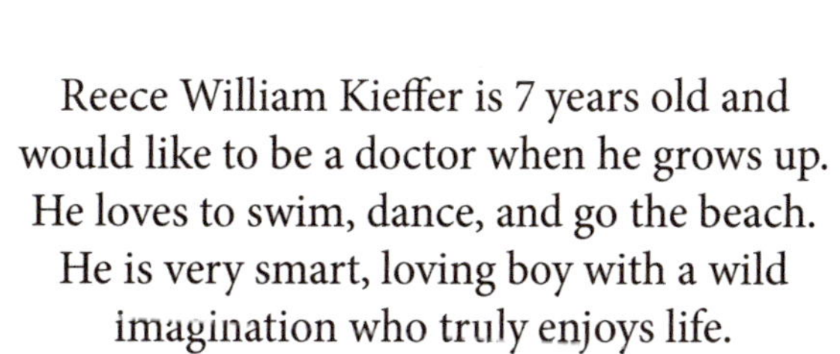

Reece William Kieffer is 7 years old and would like to be a doctor when he grows up. He loves to swim, dance, and go the beach. He is very smart, loving boy with a wild imagination who truly enjoys life.

Michael Elroy is 10 years old. He plays the piano and trombone and has acted on stage. He enjoys making videos for his YouTube channel and wants to open a technology-aimed business when he grows up. Hot chips and Mexican candy are two of his favorite things.

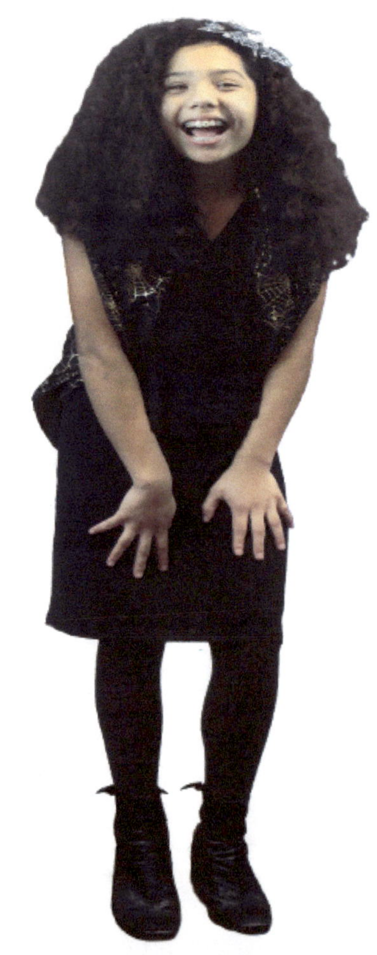

Emmalyn Truelove is 13 years old and wants to be a police officer when she grows up. She loves to sing, read, and draw. Emmalyn is an example to those who know her. She is always willing to advocate for what is right. She is kind and always willing to serve.

Nathan Housley is 6 years old and wants to be a teacher when he grows up.   He enjoys Legos and playing baseball. He is excited to be in this book with his best friend Zoe. He can't wait to share this book with his family and friends.

Cyler M. Tietgens is 9 years old and wants to be a Navy SEAL. He loves playing baseball with his friends. Cyler has a huge heart and is always willing to lend a helping hand.

Eanna B. Dunn is 8 years old and wants to be a veterinarian when she grows ups. She is very adventurous but also loves to curl up with a good book.

For My Father

For every silly, wacky, crazy world I create, please know that you will be a part of every single one. That way you will live forever in the hearts of children, as well as mine.

To order more books or submit an application to be featured in one of our upcoming books. Please visit our website WWW.CSBINNOVATIONS.COM.

www.ingramcontent.com/pod-product-compliance
Lightning Source LLC
Chambersburg PA
CBHW042112120726

47911CB00021B/140